PUFFIN BOOKS

For Rachel Spurrell and Tilly Goat.

Menaces both . . .

PUFFIN BOOKS

Published by the Penguin Group
Penguin Books Ltd, 80 Strand, London WC2R 0RL, England
Penguin Group (USA) Inc., 375 Hudson Street, New York, New York 10014, USA
Penguin Group (Canada), 90 Eglinton Avenue East, Suite 700,
Toronto, Ontario, Canada M4P 2Y3 (a division of Pearson Penguin Canada Inc.)
Penguin Ireland, 25 St Stephen's Green, Dublin 2, Ireland (a division of Penguin Books Ltd)
Penguin Group (Australia), 707 Collins Street, Melbourne, Victoria 3008, Australia
(a division of Pearson Australia Group Pty Ltd)
Penguin Books India Pvt Ltd, 11 Community Centre,
Panchsheel Park, New Delhi – 110 017, India
Penguin Group (NZ), 67 Apollo Drive, Rosedale, Auckland 0632, New Zealand
(a division of Pearson New Zealand Ltd)
Penguin Books (South Africa) (Pty) Ltd, Block D, Rosebank Office Park,
181 Jan Smuts Avenue, Parktown North, Gauteng 2193, South Africa

Penguin Books Ltd, Registered Offices: 80 Strand, London WC2R 0RL, England

puffinbooks.com

First published 2014
004

Written by Steven Butler
Illustrated by Steve May
Copyright © DC Thomson & Co. Ltd, 2014
The Beano ® ©, Dennis the Menace ® © and associated characters
TM and © DC Thomson & Co. Ltd 2013
All rights reserved

The moral right of the author, illustrator and copyright holders has been asserted

Set in Soupbone
Printed in Great Britain by Clays Ltd, St Ives plc

Except in the United States of America, this book is sold subject to the condition
that it shall not, by way of trade or otherwise, be lent, re-sold, hired out, or
otherwise circulated without the publisher's prior consent in any form of binding
or cover other than that in which it is published and without a similar condition
including this condition being imposed on the subsequent purchaser

British Library Cataloguing in Publication Data
A CIP catalogue record for this book is available from the British Library

ISBN: 978-0-141-35082-0

www.greenpenguin.co.uk

MIX
Paper from
responsible sources
FSC
www.fsc.org   FSC™ C018179

Penguin Books is committed to a sustainable
future for our business, our readers and our
planet. This book is made from paper certified
by the Forest Stewardship Council.

the Diary of Dennis the MENACE

Written by **Steven Butler**

Illustrated by **Steve May**

PUFFIN

This is the WORST day in the history of the universe ever . . . EVER!!! It's so horrible I don't think I can even write it down.

Today is

Today is the last ~~Today is the last~~

Today is the last day of

AAAAAAAAAAAaGGGGGGGHHHHHH!

OH COME ON, DENNIS . . .

Today is the LAST . . . LAST . . . LAST DAY OF THE SUMMER HOLIDAYS!

I just can't believe it. Today is my last chance for fun with Curly and Pie Face. My last day of freedom before being dragged back into Mrs Creecher's classroom and turning into a shrivelled-up Boredom Mummy for another term.

GOODBYE, CRUEL WORLD!

Today I'll eat my last meal, feed Gnasher his last bone, pick my last bogey, annoy my little sister for the last time. I'll never survive another term at schooL . . . NEVER!!

UGH!

What am I saying?

I won't survive another WEEK . . .
scratch that . . . ANOTHER DAY in Bash
Street School.

It's tooooooooooo BORING!!!

Before I know it, Boredom—Brain—Rot will
set in and I'll be done for.

There's no hope.
    School is a killer!
                I know it . . .

THE LAST WILL AND TESTAMENT OF DENNIS THE MENACE

If you're reading this, I've popped my clogs from too much **worky-boring-thinky stuff** and not enough menacing.

Curly can have my catapult and my squashed bug collection.

Pie Face can have my pea-shooter and my stripy jumper.

Mum can clean my room forever after I'm gone . . . I know she loves it.

Dad can have Gnasher . . . **MAKE SURE YOU TAKE CARE OF HIM!!**

Bea can have my Mega-Zap-Gun and my Mega-Bleep-Digi-Clock.

Oh . . . and someone smack Walter round his smarmy little face for me.

Goodbye,
from
Dead-Dennis

Me and the gang were going to head to the junkyard with my dog Gnasher and build a fort, but where am I instead? **STUCK AT HOME, THAT'S WHERE . . .**

My massive old bore of a dad went **bonkers** because I haven't done my summer homework and now he says I have to stay in until I've written it.

A diary? What kind of **evil** granny-monster of a teacher-fiend would ask a kid to write a DIARY over the **school holidays**? Only old husks like Mrs Creecher keep diaries. How am I supposed to write stuff down when I've been out menacing with Curly and Pie Face? It's a mystery to me . . .

Oh well, I've got a plan . . .

All I have to do is fill a notebook. I'll just write

really **big** . . .

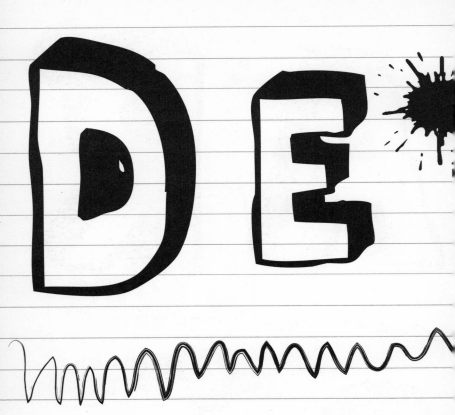

DE
DIA

ARRY

OK, so maybe that won't work. Creecher is bound to notice something.

Never mind . . . Me and the boys have done loads of brilliant things this summer . . . **LOADS!!!** Like . . . errrrm . . . Oh, like the time we put glue on the doorbell of Curly's front door. **Ha!** The milkman was stuck there for hours . . . Or the time we froze vinegar, mustard and hot, hot, **HOT** chilli powder into ice lollies and told the Softies they were tropical fruit flavour. When they tried them, their faces all puckered up like old purses. HA!!

I'll just write them down now. It will only take me a second or two . . . Old Creecher can't argue with that.

Dear Diary,

Today I got up and s~~tared at the wall.~~

Today I went and s~~tared at the wall.~~

Today I saw ~~two sticks . . . then stared at the wall.~~

Today I ate br~~eakfast while staring at the wall.~~

AAAAAAAAAAAaGGGGGGGHHHHH!

I CAN'T ADMIT

TO DOING ANY OF THE STUFF I DID

IN tHE HoLiDAys!!!

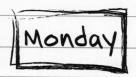

Monday

The first day back at school . . .

1 p.m.: Ugh! After the longest morning in the history of long mornings, I've got lunchtime detention . . . **Mrs Creecher just blew her wrinkly old bonce off** because I hadn't written my holiday diary. Somehow everyone else had done it. Even Curly and Pie Face! I can't believe it!

Creecher says I've got to sit in the classroom and write about how sorry I am while everyone else goes out to play.

She also says she has a private letter that she's going to personally send to Mum and Dad . . . **BIG DEAL!**

Lunchtime detention wouldn't be so bad if I couldn't see Walter and his best snob-nosed chums, Dudley and Bertie, playing on the climbing frame. If I was outside, I'd never let them on the monkey bars. They're such whopping great **know-it-all BUM-FACES!**

Ha! Bum-Faces!!

BUM-FACES! BUUUMMMM-FACES!!!!
BUM-FACES!!
BUMFACESBUMFACESBUMFACES!!
BUM-BUM-BUM-FACES!!

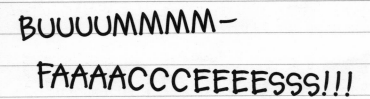

BUUUMMMM-
FAAAACCCEEEESSS!!!

BUM-FACE-BUM-FACE-BUM-FACE-

BUM-BUM-BUM-BUM-BUM-BUM-

BUM-BUMMMMMMMMMM-

BUM-BUM-BUM-

BUM-FACE-BUMMMM-

BUM-FACE-BUM-BUM-

BUM-BUM-BUM-BUM-FACE-

BUM-BUM-BUM-BUM-

BUM-FACE!!!

Ugghhff! This is awful. I should be out there, defending my title as **King of the Climbing Frame.** Up there, in my rightful spot at the top of the monkey bars, firing mud at people's bottoms with the super new catapult I made especially for the holidays.

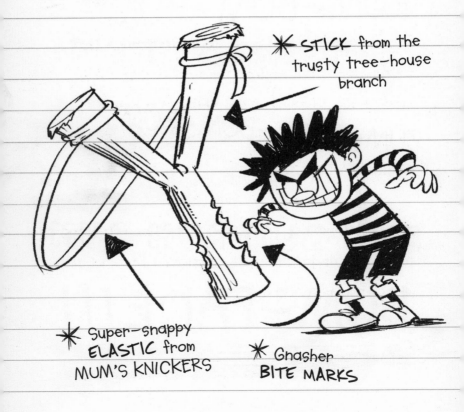

✴ STICK from the trusty tree-house branch

✴ Super-snappy ELASTIC from MUM'S KNICKERS

✴ Gnasher BITE MARKS

Instead I'm stuck by the window, watching **Walter-Wet-Pants'** gang, sitting on the monkey bars . . . **READING!** They're actually sitting there reading books at the top!! It's such a waste of a good climbing frame.

Never mind . . . All I have to do is endure this torture until the end of today and then I'll never have to think about this diary again . . . I'll be back to menacing and having fun with the gang in no time.

Ooh! I wonder what Mrs Creecher is writing to my mum and dad about, though? I know what she should be writing . . .

Dear Dennis's mum and dad,

Your son is probably a **genius** . . . probably.

If ONLY I was as clever, talented and **AMAZING** as he is.

Love from,
Wrinkly, leathery
old **Creech**

Something like that, I reckon . . .

BASH STREET

F.A.O. Dennis the Menace's Parents

It is with great disappointment that I am writing to inform you of Dennis's failure to complete his School Holiday Diary. All the other pupils in the class produced lovely accounts of their watery antics at Beanotown Lake, or hiking excursions up Mount Beano, but Dennis simply wrote: 'AAAAAAAAAAAGGGGGGHHHHHH!! I can't admit to doing any of the stuff I did in the holidays!!!'

I personally feel that an appropriate punishment should be found and would like to suggest that Dennis must now keep a diary of his entire school year as a lesson that he should always do his homework on time. I trust you'll find this suitable.

Sincerely,

Mrs Creecher

Mrs Creecher

NO! AAAAAAAAAaGGGGGHHHHHH!

It's midnight and I can't sleep . . . Every time I drop off, nightmares of getting chased by **razor-toothed, Menace-eating notebooks** flash across my brain.

This is terrible!

I CAN'T KEEP A DIARY FOR A
WHOLE SCHOOL YEAR –
I'LL TURN ALL BOOKY
LIKE CREECHER!
EVEN WORSE, I'LL TURN INTO WALTER!!

How can I waste my time worrying about
writing down what I had for breakfast and how
many fleas I found on Gnasher when there's
important menacing to be done?

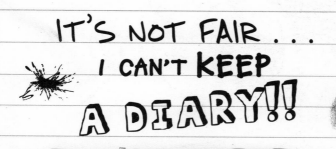

IT'S NOT FAIR . . .
I CAN'T **KEEP**
A DIARY!!

What am I going to do?

- ~~Grow a beard and run away to live in a cave on **Mount Beano**.~~

- ~~Pretend I've got **Vulture** Flu and take the whole year off school.~~

- ~~Build a **rocket-pack** out of Dad's junk in the garage and fly away.~~

- ~~**Pour glue** in Creecher's front-door lock and keep her stuck inside until she's forgotten about the holiday homework.~~

I KNOW!!

I'll train my dog **Gnasher** to eat my diary. **YES!** It's foolproof! My chomptastic best friend will eat anything. I know I can get him to eat his way through this **rotten** notebook. In fact, I'll train him to eat **every** notebook he ever sees. That way, all the notebooks in Beanotown will vanish in no time. Mrs Creecher can never blame me for not doing my homework ever again. **That'll show her!**

Tuesday

6.30 a.m.: Up bright and early thanks to my **Mega-Bleep-Digi-Clock**, and out into the garden to train Gnasher to eat diaries . . . This is going to be super easy!

GNNASH!

7 a.m.: Any minute now! Gnasher will get it . . .

7.30 a.m.: Errrrm . . .

OK, so it turns out Gnasher won't eat diaries. He's never refused food before! Maybe it's the booky—bitter taste or something. I'm going to have to rethink this one . . .

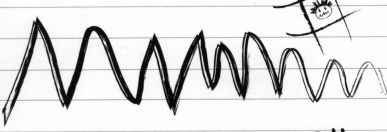

This is just too **BORING!!**
I have a **GAZILLION** menacing plots and plans and not a single . . .

WAIT A MINUTE!!!

I'VE GOT IT!

IT'S GENIUS!!

If old Creecher wants a diary, she'll get one . . .

MY KIND OF DIARY!

A DENNIS DIARY!

A MENACING

DIARY BY

DENNIS!

I'll keep a record of all the menacing that me and Gnasher get up to. It will be a **TERRIFIC** guide to being **NAUGHTY** that I'll publish all over the world and make a SQUILLION pounds!

Kids like me will read it for years to come and every good, smarty-farty, Walter-ish kid will learn how to menace like a proper . . . umm . . . **MENACE**! Even Creecher will stop her terrible learny ways and join my Menace Squad. **I'll think of it as a menacing manual to teach all future Menaces how to do it properly . . .**

Especially my little sister Bea. It's important that someone carries on the fine family tradition.

Wednesday

8 a.m.: Heading to Bash Street School with my new, brilliant Menacing Diary. I'm feeling more inspired than ever. I've got a whole lot of new ideas to cause some chaos in class.

Going to drop in to **Mr Har Har's Joke Shop** on the way. That's always a good place to spend your pocket money and pick up some essential supplies for the term ahead.

Must buy:

✳ Fake spider with jiggly legs

◉ Itching powder

✳ Exploding candy

◉ Snap-bangers

There are lots of other important things you'll need to get your grabbers on if you want to be a **true Menace** . . .

MENACING SUPPLIES

Mum's camera: it's important to **document all tricks** played on Softies. That way you'll always have something to bribe or embarrass them with.

Pram wheels: from little sisters' pushchairs or from the junkyard. **Very important for go-carts.**

Rotten tomatoes and mud pies: for catapult ammo.

Old hosepipes: for spraying unsuspecting Softies.

String: great for **tripwires** and dangling fake spiders from a height.

Pencil and paper: all good tricks start with a well-written note.

Snacks: because menacing on an empty stomach can be a very dangerous business indeed.

Straws: they make great emergency **pea-shooters**.

old clothes from Mum and Dad's wardrobe: a good Menace always has a **disguise** or two up his or her sleeve.

Banana skins: great as a quick slippery trap.

Knicker elastic: important if you want to have the snappiest catapult in Beanotown.

Go AND GET COLLECTING
NOW!!

This is going to be the best term
ever now I've got my new mission, and
I know exactly how I'm going to kick
it into action . . .

I've got a trick up my sleeve, but
before I tell you, you need to know a
few menacing basics . . .

HOW TO BE A MASTER OF MENACING!!

This is no easy business. You've got to be prepared and ready for action and know when to seize the right menacing moment. Then there are the ten RULES . . . Never, **EVER FORGET THOSE!!**

Copy them down . . .

Keep them with you at all times . . .

BUT . . .

NEVER LET THEM FALL INTO ENEMY HANDS!!

The Rules of MENACING!

RULE 1: Always be ready to menace. Grab the opportunity and don't look back.

RULE 2: Never menace while carrying scissors.

RULE 3: In the case of an emergency, laugh really hard, then run like the wind.

RULE 4: Steer clear of grown-ups: they're tricky.

RULE 5: SAY NO TO SCHOOLWORK!

Paper is not for books and writing! It is for squidging up into little balls with your spit and firing at the back of your teacher's head with your pea-shooter.

RULE 6: Don't forget your pea-shooter.

RULE 7: Never, never, **NEVER** leave home without your catapult.

RULE 8: Get a dog. All Menaces must have one. Abyssinian wire-haired tripe hounds like Gnasher are the **BEST!**

RULE 9: Don't trust anyone more than your dog. A good Menace's dog is worth its weight in sweets and crisps and pocket money.

BuT!!!!

The **tenth** most biggest whopping great rule of menacing that you must never, never, ever forget:

DRUM
ROLL
PLEASE!!

WATCH

FOR

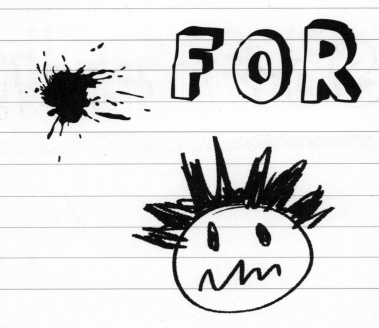

OUT

SOFTIES!!

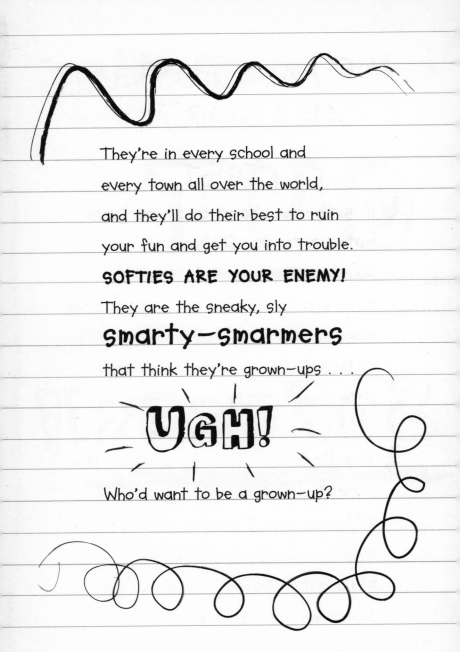

They're in every school and
every town all over the world,
and they'll do their best to ruin
your fun and get you into trouble.

SOFTIES ARE YOUR ENEMY!

They are the sneaky, sly
smarty-smarmers
that think they're grown-ups . . .

UGH!

Who'd want to be a grown-up?

ARE YOU A MENACE OR A SOFTY?

TEST

1 It's the weekend and you have nothing to do. Do you:

a) Steal the wheels from your little sister's pram and make a go-cart to race down the biggest hill in Beanotown?

b) Do some spring-cleaning with your little squirrel and bluebird friends?

2 You find ten whole pounds in the street. Do you:

a) Run straight to Mr Har Har's Joke Shop and buy menacing supplies?

b) Hand it to Sergeant Slipper at the Beanotown Police Station?

3 Mum and Dad want to take you to watch the ballet Duck Lake. Do you:

a) Fake a terrible disease, using Mum's red lipstick to draw on spots and a can of vegetable soup as extra-realistic sick, and not go?

b) Go to the ballet and love every minute of it . . . especially the delicate steps and wafty music?

4 Mum and Dad buy you a dog for your birthday. Do you:

a) Name it Biter, Cruncher, Drooler, Killer, Nipper, Scratcher or Stinker?

b) Name it Fwuffy, Petal, Beauty, Cutie, Daisy, Maisy?

5 Look at this picture of Walter . . .

Do you:

a) Think it's a bum and want to cover it up quickly with a pair of pants?

b) Think he looks like a 'spiffy chap' and want to get to know him?

RIGHT!

PENCILS DOWN, PLEASE . . .

LOOK AT YOUR ANSWERS . . .

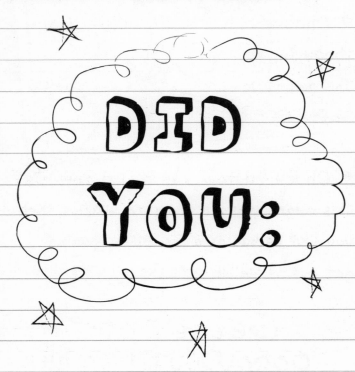

DID YOU:

- Choose only **A**s the whole way through the test?

This means you are a true Menace and one of the coolest, bestest people ever to walk the earth, EVER!

- Choose only **B**s the whole way through the test?

This means you are a stinky, wet-panted Softy. GET OUT!!!!

- Choose a few **A**s and a few **B**s?

This means you are not sure, which makes you just as bad as a Softy so you can get out as well!!!

GEEEETTTT OOOOUUUUTTTT!!!!

OK, if you've got this far, hopefully you are already well on your way to becoming an expert Menace. But there are still some things you've got to be careful about . . .

How to Spot a Softy

1 **A SOFTY** is an unpredictable, diabolical Mister Maturity . . . Listen out for the smarmish, mature things they say. It's a sure-fire sign that you're dealing with a

booky-boring-bonce!

2 Are they carrying a book about QUANTUM PHYSICS, THE LIFE OF SLOW—GROWING WEEDS AND FUNGUS or STAMP COLLECTING FOR EXPERTS? In fact, are they carrying a book at all? If they are, they're probably a Softy.

3 Do they dress like a smelly, geeky computer nerd? All Softies do . . .

WATCH OUT!

4 Do they make you want to be sick and then throw boulders and anything else that's lying around at them, every time you look at them? **Yes?**

That's a Softy for sure!!

My archest enemy is WALTER. Look at him . . .

READING GLASSES for extra-boring books

SMARMY SMILE

BUM-FACE

Devious knees

Old grandad SHOES

He is the leader of the Softy gang here in Beanotown and I'll bet he's already smugging his way around, thinking of ways to get me into even more trouble than I'm already in. I'll show him and old Creecher. They won't know what's hit 'em . . .

Anyway, in case you forgot, I said I had a trick up my sleeve . . .

If you're going to learn how to be a Menace like me, you must always listen to what I tell you. After all, I am the **PRANKMASTER GENERAL**!!

Last term, on the final day of school, Headmaster sent us off on our summer holiday with a long, boring speech about planning ahead and saving for a rainy day.

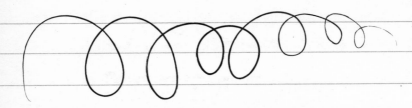

So I DID...

I've been saving up an amazing trick for weeks. I knew Walter would need a bit of a boot in the backside at some point and now I've decided to start the new term and my new Menacing Diary by putting this super-secret operation into action.

Here's the plan:

Top-secret Trickery
OPERATION
GROUCHY GROWN-UP

My next-door neighbour is a grumpy old groucher. **THE GRUMPIEST OLD GROUCHER!!** Here he is . . .

THE COLONEL

Since the start of the holidays, I have set my **Mega-Bleep-Digi-Clock** to wake me up at **5 a.m.** EVERY morning. Then I'd creep outside, climb over the garden fence to the Colonel's house and ring his doorbell.

As soon as I heard the old grump yelling and clattering to his bedroom window shouting, **'BE OFF WI' YER!!!'**, I'd shoot straight back over the fence and off to bed before he could catch me.

He's been going crackers and sloshing his washing-up bowl out the window over the last few weeks, but I'm always too quick and already back in my garden and hidden from sight by the time he does . . . **HA!**

Today, in class, I'm going to slip a note to
Walter . . .

> Attention, Walter!
>
> March over to my house at **5 a.m.**
> tomorrow! There's something very
> hush-hush I have to brief you on. Vital to
> the security of the country. Bound to
> be on the front page of *The Beanotown
> Bugle* when the mission's over. You'll be
> up for a medal, old chap!
>
> Toodlepip,
>
> # The Colonel

It's too funny to be true!! I managed to stuff
the note into Walter's maths book when he was
off crawling round Mrs Creecher at lunchtime.

Then in the playground I heard . . .

HE FELL FOR IT!!

I can't wait for **5 a.m.** tomorrow morning . . .

This is going to be hilarious!!!

BLEEP . . . BLEEEPPP . . .
BLEEEEPPPP!!!

4.45 a.m.: Oh, it's early, but me and Gnasher are up in the tree house ready for Walter to arrive. I feel like a secret agent! We've got a perfect view from here. I wish I'd brought some popcorn. HA!

4.48 a.m.: Walter always arrives early. Where is he?

4.51 a.m.: The waiting is UNBEARABLE!! Gnasher's getting restless and my bum is getting cold. I REALLY, REALLY wish I'd brought some popcorn!

4.52 a.m.: HE'S HERE!! I knew Wet–Lettuce–Walter would be early. This is Secret Agent Dennis signing out . . .

Check . . .

check . . .

over . . .

 check!

5.15 a.m.: That was the best thing I HAVE EVER SEEN!! You should have been here – you would have laughed until you wet yourself! Walter showed up, dressed in his bow tie and humming to himself about a medal. Then . . . when he rang the doorbell, the Colonel was ready and waiting as usual.

Walter ran home like a stale old biscuit that had been dunked in tea for too long, and me and Gnasher nearly fell out of the tree house, we hooted so much. I can't wait to tell Walter that *I* wrote the note at school later. What a brilliant start to my new

MENACING YEAR!!

WARNING!

IF YOU READ ANY FURTHER,

YOU WILL PROBABLY BE SICK

FROM LAUGHING SO HARD

AND TURN INTO A MASTER OF

MENACING IN NO TIME FLAT!!

Friday . . . or is it Thursday? Not sure

My stonking great trick on Walter was just the beginning of the amazing things I've got planned for the new school term and the start of your training as the next generation of Menaces.

You've got so much to learn but, lucky for you, I'm feeling very wise in the ways of mischief today . . . Hmmm, we'd better crack on . . . We've done the rules and I've warned you about the Softies.
What next?

Aha!! I know!! If you're going to be **MASTERS OF MENACING** like me and Gnasher, you've got to know all the hiding places, escape routes, lookouts, dead ends, pitfalls, hideouts and vantage points in your neighbourhood.

Take Beanotown, for instance. If your town is anything like mine, it'll be full of brilliant places to help you menace. I'll show you around . . .

THE TREE HOUSE

TOP-SECRET hideout for all Menaces everywhere

A GREAT VIEW of the Colonel's and Walter's houses

Perfect place to stash TOP-SECRET THINGS like chocolate and pocket money

Every good Menace has to have a base, and the best menacing bases are tree houses. It's amazing what funny things you can see from the top of a tree and, if Softies are sniffing about, you just have to pull up the ladder and they can't get anywhere near you, keeping you and your top-secret plans safe from snoopy, piggy eyes.

BeanoTown Park

A squillion HIDING PLACES

Parks are a great stomping ground for
Menaces. Beanotown Park is full of trees for
climbing and hiding in, and has the boating
pond and playground. The climbing frame in the
playground is a fantastic lookout for keeping an

SWINGS (not very useful, but super fun)

BEWARE OF THE DUCK!

The BOATING POND for fishing, swimming and splashing SOFTIES

eye on Walter and his cronies and, if you need to top up your **MENACE−OMETER**, you can push them in the pond. Walter is terrified of pondweed and screams like a whingey baby every time . . . **Ha!**

BASH STREET SCHOOL

Now wait a minute!! I know what you're thinking . . . School? **Has Dennis gone loopy?**

No! Dennis hasn't gone LOOPY! Think of all the great menacing supplies that are there for the taking. PAINT, INK, MODELLING CLAY, PAPER, CHALK, DRAWING PINS!! Never underestimate the importance of a quick, secret trip to the school stock cupboard.

REMEMBER!

MENACES MEAN BUSINESS –
STOCK UP NOW!!!!

THE JUNKYARD

A treasure trove of MENACING SUPPLIES

What can I say? The junkyard is the

COOLEST place in the universe.

GRAN'S HOUSE

Features:

● Cake

● Biscuits

● CAKE!!!

OK, so not everyone is lucky enough to have a gran like mine. My gran is a menacing mastermind and rides around town on her **Charley Davidson** motorcycle with her pets **Gnipper** the dog and **Rasher** the pig. Other grans are just a bit forgetful and smell of wee and bug spray . . . **BUT!!** Grannies always have cake and biscuits, and Menaces need to eat. It's a good place to stop off in the middle of an adventure, for a quick snack or two . . . or five . . .

BASH STREET KIDS

Fatty

Danny

Toots

Plug

Wilfrid

Smiffy

Spotty

'Erbert

Sidney

No matter how good a Menace you are, sometimes you need a little help. Bash Street is the home of a bunch of great Menaces that are always glad to help out in moments of dire need.

NEVER UNDERESTIMATE THE HANDINESS OF FELLOW MENACES!!

NUMBER 13
FRIGHTVILLE AVENUE

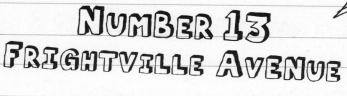

Spiders

Ghosts

Every town has a **scary house** that no one wants to go near — and Number 13 Frightville Avenue is scarier than most. A quick double-dare for someone to go up the path and knock on the front door is a sure-fire way to separate the **Menaces** from the **Softies** ...

Oh, and speaking of scary things, it's

Halloween in a month or so . . . I want to go as

DENNISTEIN!!
or
FRANKEN-MENACE!!

I haven't decided which yet.

Just saying . . .

It was rainy at the weekend, and Mum said I had to stay indoors and play with my little sister Bea or I couldn't have ice cream after dinner. Parents are so EVIL sometimes . . .

BEA

CAN YOU IMAGINE? ME?

PLAYING WITH . . . BEA?

Bea's all right if you need someone to crawl under the fence and bring back a ball, or if you need to use her as an emergency stink bomb in a moment of panic . . . But making me play with her when I should be out exploring Beanotown Forest with Curly and Pie Face is just plain cruel. **SHE WANTED ME TO PLAY DOLLS!!!**

Still, it wasn't all bad, I guess. Bea got in a mega-strop because I fed her stupid doll to Gnasher . . . He loves the taste of toys.

Well, what was I **supposed** to do? Anyway, I saved one of its legs for her to play with. What's so bad about that?

Before long, her face got all red and frowny, and anyone who's met Bea knows what 'red-faced and frowny' means . . .

Sure enough, she let rip the biggest, stinkiest, eye-wateringest blow-off you've EVER heard. It was so **DISGUSTING** that Gnasher started howling!! I'm surprised the wallpaper didn't peel off!! It even made the windows rattle . . .

BRRRRP!

Who knew a stinky little sister could be so useful?

REMEMBER . . .

EVEN HORRIBLE LITTLE SISTERS HAVE THEIR USES . . .
SOMETIMES . . .

In no time at all we had to evacuate the house with hankies tied over our noses and mouths, but it was still raining outside. We stood there for ages, huddled on the front step like soggy lumps of misery, until Mum and Dad finally gave in. We couldn't possibly go back indoors for at least another few hours, so they bundled us into the car and drove out to get some dinner while the stink went away back at home.

Mum wanted to go to her favourite restaurant,
La Frenchie Pu-Pu, but Bea and I kicked up
a fuss in the back seat and we went to OUR
favourite restaurant instead: **BEANOTOWN
BURGERS!**

It's the best restaurant in
the universe!

I had the Slopper-Gnosher-Gut-Bustin' Burger with Super-Loop Chips and EXTRA tomato sauce.

Cheesy Bun

Tomato Sauce

Lettuce

Cheese

More Cheese

Onion Rings

Fatty Salted Crispies

Crispy Salted Fatties

Even More Cheese

Beefburger

Bun

It's my favourite out of all the mega-burgers at Beanotown Burgers.

If I could, I'd eat Slopper-Gnosher-Gut-Bustin' Burgers and Super-Loop Chips for every meal . . . **EVEN BREAKFAST** . . . But Dad says I'd get fat like the people on TV.

Hmmmmm . . . Imagine how happy all those fat people around the world must be. Sigh!

Thursday

Ha! Walter actually cried in class today . . . **ACTUALLY CRIED!!**

Guess why??

He found out about my diary punishment from Creecher and thinks it's not fair because he wants to write one. He actually WANTS extra homework!! Even Mrs Creecher looked shocked, so she let him write one too. I think she only did it to shut him up!

Walter's diary . . . I can just imagine it . . .

84

DEAR DIARY,

I AM WALTER THE BUM-FACE.
I AM THE BIGGEST BUM-FACE IN
ALL THE LAND AND ONE DAY I'LL
BE KING OF THE BUM-FACES AND
EVERYONE WILL CALL ME 'KING
BUM-FACE THE SMARMY' . . .

THE END

The Next Wednesday

Today is a super-exciting day.

It's been rainy for ages, and weeks, and months, and FOREVER, and we've had to have 'wet playtime' inside. Everyone hates rainy breaks. You just have to stay in the classroom like it's normal school time and not a real break at all.

BUT, finally, it's dry outside and you know what that means???

Oh, wait . . . no you don't!

WOW!

I hadn't realized just how much you've still got
to learn about being a Menace.

Let me explain, my Menacing Mates . . .

Every day (so long as it's dry out), when
the first morning break comes at **11 a.m.,**
the bell rings and there's a mad race out of
the classroom, across the playground, over
the wobbly manhole cover, hurdling the picnic
benches, round the old tree, to the climbing
frame at the edge of the Bash Street School
footy field.

Turn over for
my secret map!

School

PLAYGROUND

Wobbly
manhole
cover

The first kid to reach the top of the monkey
bars is **KING FOR THE REST OF
THE DAY** and can order everyone else
about. It's BRILLIANT!! Whenever I win (AND

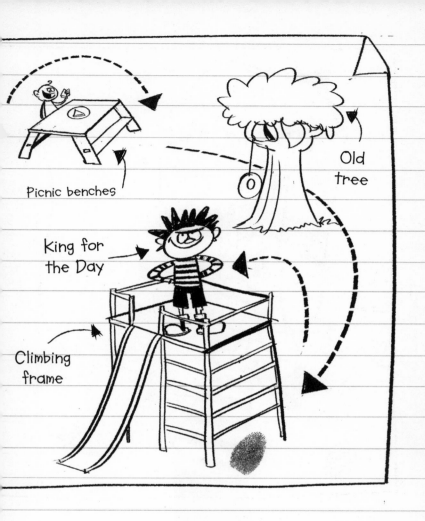

Picnic benches

Old tree

King for the Day

Climbing frame

I WIN A LOT), I like to send people off on errands and then, when they're walking away, fire mud balls at their backsides with my trusty catapult. HA!

It's not always that simple, though. My biggest threat, when it comes to King of the Climbing Frame, is **Minnie the Minx.**

She's the **biggest minx** at Bash Street
School and can run just as fast as any of the
boys. Odds are, if I'm not King of the Climbing
Frame, it's because Minnie has tripped me up
or set a trap, and I have to put up with the
TORTURE of being bossed around by Queen
Smell-izabeth the First for the whole day.

It makes me
SOOOO MAD
when Minnie wins!!

INVENTION:
The Lady Launcher

1 Minnie runs across the playground

2 Steps on manhole cover

3 A giant spring from the junkyard is released

It's always been the same . . . ALWAYS!

People have been fighting to be King of the Climbing Frame in Beanotown ever since the caveman days.

IT'S TRUE! Trust me, I know . . .

Last year, Headmaster took us on the **BORING—BORING—BORINGEST** school trip to Beanotown Museum.
It was **SOOOOO bad!**

What are museums for? Why do we need to go to museums just to see that people back in the olden days were really boring, and didn't have TVs, and liked to use lots of broken brown clay pots? I tell you, they're everywhere!

It's like a plague! You can't turn round in a museum without bumping into a shelf covered in bits of old brown clay pot . . . Zzzzzz!!!

Anyway . . . there was a room at the back of the museum filled with lumpy wax models of cavemen all sitting round a fire in a cave. Walter cried because he thought they looked scary, but I thought they looked like Mrs Creecher with a beard!!

At first I felt sure I was going to explode from boringness, but **THEN** I saw the cave painting on the wall above. It was of a funny little man standing at the top of a pile of sticks, waving his little arms like he was celebrating. Headmaster told us it was a picture of 'a man gathering wood for a fire', but I knew the truth.

It was obvious! That little cave-painting man had just beaten all the other cave-painting men to the top of their cavey climbing frame and was **KING** for the day . . . Terrific!!

AND, if you don't believe me, you can go and read Walter's diary instead. That'll be fun! You'll soon miss me . . .

Anyway . . . Morning break is in ten minutes and I can't wait to see who's King or Queen today.

YEAH!! OF COURSE I WON!

Hmmmph!

Minnie won . . . It's not fair!

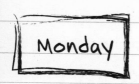

Monday

Walter is STILL writing in his
STOOOPID diary . . .

I can't stop staring – it's fascinating. He sits
there at lunchtime with his fancy–schmancy
notebook with a big gold lock on it and giggles
to himself like a demented elf.

I wonder what he's writing in there.

Dear Dennis,

Thank you so much for writing AGAIN . . .
As I've told you many times before,
it is not possible for us to package and
mail Walter to Papua New Guinea or the
moon. What is a Walter? Is it a person?
I understand from your letter that Walter
is a bum-face, but we really can't post
humans overseas.
Please don't ask again as it upsets
the postmen and women.
Have you tried a furniture
removal company?

Yours wearily,

G. Gooper

Gladys Gooper
Postmistress
Beanotown Post Office

Tuesday

I AM A GENIUS!!

I GOT WALTER'S DIARY . . . well . . . part of it. We were in the canteen at school and Walter was being all secretive in the corner as usual, writing in his diary and giggling to himself.

Let me tell you, there's nothing more annoying than the sound of his snorty little laugh, so I got Pie Face to go and tell him that they were serving super-expensive 'EL SNOBBO CAVIAR' at the lunch counter . . . AND . . . Walter shot off like a wafty firework, shouting, **'OOOH, MY FAVOURITE KIND!'**

I was going to snatch the entire diary, but Walter kept twirling and turning round on his way over to the dinner lady and he would have seen me, so I just opened it and ripped out as many pages as I could.

Most of it was wimpy rubbish like . . .

Oh, how I long for a meadow stroll!

It's enough to make anyone sick . . . and there was this . . . **Boring!**

Dearest Diary-poos,

Today I shampooed my darling cat, Claudius. He's such a good boy. He's sooooo good he's PURRR-FECT!! HAHAHA! Sometimes I'm so funny I could just burst!

BUT THEN I FOUND THIS!

I knew that weasel was up to something . . .

Dearest, dearest Diary,

It's me, your best friend in the whole wide world, Walter. Oh, how I've missed writing on your silken pages. How long has it been now? Twenty minutes? It's been unbearably miserable.

I have a secret for you, my wondrous little diary friend. It's all about Dennis. He's the one I told you about . . . you know, the one with that horrible, drooling dog that's completely ruining our pleasant, lovely neighbourhood.

OH, I CAN'T WAIT TO WRITE THIS NEXT LINE . . . MY HEART IS PRACTICALLY ALL AFLUTTER!!

We're going to get him!

There! I said it! Bertie, Dudley and I are going to get that monstrous hooligan once and for all. Pretty soon Dennis shall menace his last menace and never come out of his nasty little home again . . .

Here's the plan, my best diary pal: in two days it's Halloween and, after that terrible trick that Dennis pulled on me with the invite to the Colonel's house, I thought it was high time I repaid him. Bertie, Dudley and I are going to send an anonymous invitation to Dennis and his two dim-witted friends, Curly and Pie Face, asking them to attend a Gala Costume Party at Number 13 Frightville Avenue. It's the scariest old house in all of Beanotown. Even Dennis is nervous about that place. AND . . . we'll be waiting for him.

When he arrives and knocks on the door, we'll all jump out and make him scream like a Whingey-Wilfred and he'll be so embarrassed, he'll never show his face in town again.

It's splendid!

So the Softies think they can outsmart Dennis the Menace, do they? I'm surprised Walter would even dare to think about going into Number 13. I have to hand it to him, it is a pretty scary place . . . That's quite a good menace . . . for a Softy!!

I've got a trick up my jumper sleeve. This is going to be the best Halloween **EVER!!!**

Not Sure What Day It Is

Ha! Walter has been going round school all morning talking about a costume party at 13 Frightville Avenue for only the **COOLEST** guests, and how sorry he is that he hasn't been invited. If only that little grub knew that I'm already on to him . . . He'd eat his bow tie in anger.

Later the Same Day

It arrived! Look what I found waiting on my desk after lunch . . .

Dearest Dennis,

You are hereby invited to attend the best, grandest, most marvellous, cool, cooler, coolest Gala Costume Party in the world EVER! Please come to 13 Frightville Avenue at 7.30 p.m. and don't be late . . . YOU'RE ALWAYS LATE!
And bring those two friends of yours . . . and that dog. And don't be late . . . Oh – and wear a costume.

Signed,
Anonymous . . .

PS Don't be late.

Ha! It's all set . . . I ran up to Walter and waved my invitation in his face and pretended I was super excited. I even convinced him that I was still going to dress up as **Dennistein** for the party. Now he thinks he's got us, and we're going to show up at the front door of 13 Frightville Avenue and get the scare of our lives. BUT things are going to happen a little differently.

It won't be me and the boys that are scared out of our pants on Halloween. That weaselly little snobber will wet his frilly knickers before I'm done with him.

I've got work to do . . .

OPERATION TERROR-TRICK:
Things we're going to need . . .

☆ One of Mum's extra-white bedsheets

☆ The broom from Dad's shed

☆ The mop from the kitchen

☆ My Mighty-Mouth-Megaphone

☆ The lids from the Colonel's bins

☆ If Walter wants to play haunted house, he's going to get one. It's super easy to make a good ghost . . .
I'll show you!

X-Ray Ghost

It's all set. Tomorrow, after school, me and the boys are going to dash across town, sneak into Number 13 long before Walter gets there and hide, ready to give him a fright he'll never forget.

HALLOWEEN

6.30 p.m.: OK, we're here . . . Gnasher managed to crunch his way through the padlock on the back door and we got inside just in time before Walter and his cronies appeared at the bottom of the path.

It was so funny watching them from the window at the top of the stairs.

At first they were all too scared to even come near the house and kept taking a few steps through the gate, screaming, and running back out again. They plucked up the courage eventually. **WOW!** Those Softies must really want to trick me . . .

I can hear them whispering downstairs.

This is going to be **FANTASTIC!**

It's really creepy in here, though. I hope
there are no ghosts.

6.50 p.m.: It's almost time. Curly is poised in
the bushes out the front of the house, and Pie
Face has crammed himself inside the cupboard
under the stairs with the Colonel's dustbin lids.
All me and Gnasher have to do is wait . . .

6.55 p.m.: Aaaaaagh! I'm so excited –
I can't wait to see Walter's face!

At 7.30 p.m. exactly Curly is going to
knock on the front door, then hide. When the

Softies answer it and find there's no one there, they'll freak out for sure. Then Pie Face will start clattering the bin lids and making thunder noises, while Gnasher and me give the ghostly performance of a lifetime . . .

I WANT MY MUMMY!

There's no one there!

Two Minutes Later: AMAZING!

The trick worked perfectly . . . Walter was screaming and ran outside so fast his bow tie was spinning like a propeller. If only he'd stay inside his house and never come out again, like he thought I was going to.

HAPPY HALLOWEEN,

TRAINEE MENACES . . .

THERE'S PLENTY MORE WHERE THAT CAME FROM!

Friday

Wowzers! That was my best Halloween
yet. I still haven't stopped laughing to myself.
I don't even mind that I didn't get to dress up
as Dennistein in the end. It was all worth it . . .

Monday

Still laughing to myself . . . Mrs Creecher
yelled at me today for snickering in class, but
I don't care. I can still picture Walter, Bertie
and Dudley wetting their pants as they ran off
home to their mummies. Oh, the joy!

FOUND: stuck on a lamp-post in our street.

MISSING!
Two lovely metal bin lids.

Last seen on the morning of Halloween.

If anyone has seen or heard anything,

please contact the Colonel.

£1 reward.

Life COULDN'T be sweeter. As if the amazingness of Halloween wasn't enough fun to last a lifetime, it's Bonfire Night!! I'm so excited. Me and the boys are heading down to Beanotown Park after school. Parky Bowles the park keeper is putting on his usual firework display. Gugh!! **I LOVE FIREWORKS!!**

Last year, Parky spent days piling up wood and twigs to make the massive bonfire big enough for the night. And . . . every day before school, and while Parky was off collecting branches, Curly and Pie Face would dare me to sneak down to the big pile and stuff snap-bangers into the gaps. **IT WOULD HAVE BEEN BRILLIANT!**

By Bonfire Night, we'd have put squillions of snap-bangers in there! **Enough to make it take off like a rocket!!**

Imagine how amazing it would be to see your local community bonfire take off and fly out of town like it didn't approve of the neighbourhood.

BUT WE NEVER GOT THE CHANCE!!
BOG-FACED OLD PARKY checks the bonfire every single day to make sure no one has put snap-bangers in it! He probably has a wheelie bin full of confiscated snap-bangers somewhere (what a firework that would be)!

IT'S NOT FAIR!!

But . . . I CAN'T WAIT FOR TONIGHT!!

I've got big, **BIG plans . . .**

So . . . I was thinking I might trick Walter into believing he's part of an **AMAZING** new science project to put the world's first genius on the moon. He's bound to fall for that! Then all I have to do is strap a **GIANT** whizz-rocket to his back and stick the end of the extra-long fuse into the big pile of sticks.

When Parky Bowles lights the bonfire, the whole thing will go up like a comet in a bow tie and we'll never see or hear from Walter-Wimp-Sniffle again . . .

Sounds perfect . . . No?

Oh, wait . . .

OH NO!!

AAAAAAAAAAAAGGGGGGGHHHHHH!

Look what I've just seen pinned to the school
noticeboard . . .

BASH STREET

Dear Pupils,

I regret to inform you that tonight's firework
display in Beanotown Park has been cancelled
due to a FREAK SNOWSTORM that is heading
directly for us.

   Please head straight home at the end of
school and wrap up warm. The next few days
are going to be very cold indeed.

Yours truly,

Headmaster

Headmaster

UGH! So much for launching Walter into orbit. I was so excited . . .

ARTIST'S IMPRESSION

Oh well, there's always next year . . . AND IT'S NOT SO BAD . . . SNOW!!! I LOVE SNOW!!!

I CAN'T WAIT . . . MAYBE SCHOOL WILL BE CLOSED FOR A FEW DAYS???

I'm off home . . .

123

I FOUND MY DIARY!!

YEAH!!!!

Thursday

After all that searching round the house, it turned out that Bea had my diary stashed under her playpen. It has been missing for **WEEKS!!!** She must have grabbed it from my room when I wasn't looking and was using it as a colouring book, the little Menace. **Ha!** She takes after her brother after all.

WOWZERS! YOU'VE GOT SO MUCH TO CATCH UP ON!!

So, you remember the letter on the school noticeboard about the freak snowstorm?

Of course you do . . .

Well, it turned out to be the **BIGGEST** blizzard that Beanotown has EVER seen!! We had so much snow that Dad had to dig his way out of our front door. It was **BRILLIANT!!** All we could see was his head, bobbing around above the snowline.

School has been closed for weeks and it's been BRILLIANT!!! We didn't even see the last day of term. Headmaster must have been completely lost. I bet he didn't know what to do with himself when he couldn't give us his usual jabbery speech about this and that and such-'n'-such . . .

Life COULDN'T BE BETTER!

No homework!
No spelling tests!

Instead of our last day of school, we all trudged out into the streets and had a snowman competition.

It was brilliant . . . Walter thinks his snowman was best, but I know mine was . . . **definitely!**

It's been so much fun . . . This is what life should be like all the time. Who needs school?

OUT OF ALL THE THINGS RUINED BY THE SNOW, BEST OF ALL IS . . . NO END-OF-TERM CAROL CONCERT!!

It's the worst. Every year, right before the end of term, Creecher makes us stand up at the front of the school hall and sing a load of boring old songs for our parents. Can you imagine the humiliation, having to stand there singing while Mum cries and Dad films you on his video camera? It's torture! It's torture on film that they make you watch again and again each Christmas . . .

BUT NOT THIS YEAR!

Old Creech can stand in the middle of her living room and sing her own carols to herself!

Jingle bells,

Creecher smells,

Of bug spray and of wee.

Santa Claus

Got such a shock,

Coming down her chim—a—nee!

OH!

 Jingle bells,

Creecher smells,

So Santa ran away.

Now she won't have any gifts

To open, Christmas Day!

HEY!

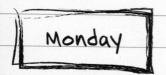

Monday

Well, my Menacing Mates, I can't believe we made it this far. A whole term at Bash Street School!

It's Christmas in just two days . . . The funnest, craziest, most menacy time of year in our house.

We're not quite done yet, though. There's plenty of menacing to get in before that happens.

I have one word for you . . .

GRAN!

The absolute best-bester-bestest thing about Christmas is when my gran comes round for Christmas dinner. She's the coolest old biddy this side of Mount Beano. I can't wait to see what she gets up to this year.

Dear Santa,

It's **Dennis** . . . I've been very extra good this year and . . . Well, all right, I haven't been that good, but it's not my fault. I go to school with some complete **BUM-FACES** and, if I didn't do the odd menace here and there, they'd swell and grow until they were the world's biggest **BUM-FACES**. So, in a way, playing tricks on Walter and his cronies makes me super-extra good.

Anyway, I was thinking . . .

I know you're a cool guy and I'm pretty sure you would think Walter was top of the **ANNOYING LIST**, so I was wondering if you'd help me out?

I bet you have mounds and mounds of reindeer poo up in the North Pole and you don't know what to do with it. Well, Santa, it's your lucky day . . . Take a look at this!

It would make my Christmas if you would bring all that poo to Beanotown and dump it on Walter's house . . . He would get the shock of his life and you wouldn't have to climb over mountains of reindeer poo every day . . . **Ahhh,** what a lovely Christmas present that would be for both of us? No?

I know you can do it, Santa . . .

From

Dennis

Christmas Eve

AAAAAAAAAAAGGGGGGHHHHHH!

Christmas Eve is the **Best** and the **Worst Day Ever.** It's so exciting that Santa is coming from the North Pole tonight, but it's so annoying that it's not Christmas Day yet.

Tomorrow is going to be **SOOOO** menacy, I can tell. After my letter to Santa, he's bound to bring me more presents than anyone else in the world this year . . . **sigh** . . . I can just see it now . . .

I'll wake up to the sound of Mum and Dad squabbling over who is going to cook the roast potatoes, and the

CRUNCH CRUNCH CRUNCH

of Gnasher chewing the trunk of the Christmas tree. Then I'll roll over AND . . . that's when I'll see it . . .

A STOCKING, SO BIG IT FILLS UP

MY ENTIRE BEDROOM!!

There'll be toys everywhere. MORE TOYS THAN I CAN COUNT (AND I CAN COUNT REALLY HIGH).

It's going to be **AMAZING!!**

Lunchtime: Snowball fight with Curly and Pie Face . . . Agh! It's not going quick enough. I CAN'T WAIT FOR TOMORROW.

4 p.m.: Trying not to think about tomorrow. It's driving me **CRAZY** with excitement . . . Heading home for dinner. (Might go past Walter's house on the way and knock the head off his snowman . . . BRILLIANT!)

5 p.m.: Ugh! Bea won't leave me alone. She wants me to play with her doll again. This one wets itself if you pull its hair . . . Weird!

I'm too busy waiting for Christmas Day to play with her. When she wasn't looking, I shoved her doll inside the Christmas turkey on the kitchen table. Mum's defrosting it for dinner tomorrow . . .

It's HUGE!

6 p.m.: I've buried my Mega-Bleep-Digi-Clock under my bed. I can't stop checking it.

8 p.m.: I can't take it any more . . . If Christmas Day doesn't come soon, my head will

EXPLODE!!

I'll go put my fake plastic spider with jiggly legs in one of Mum's slippers to take my mind off it . . .

Right! It's getting late. I'm off to bed. **Fingers crossed for tomorrow . . .**

CHRISTMAS DAY!!!

7 a.m.: I can't look!! I'm under the blanket as we speak . . .

I can hear Mum and Dad squabbling . . .

I can hear Gnasher chewing the tree . . .

It's all coming true!! My giant stocking with a **GAZILLION** presents must be there!!

OK . . . I'm going to take a peek.

Three . . .

 Two . . .

 One . . .

143

This is TERRIBLE!!

I know I've been a Menace this year, but Santa was supposed to understand and leave me loads of cool things. All I got was a measly, normal-sized stocking on the end of my bed with some stripy socks and a Beanotown United footy scarf in it . . .

I just checked out the window and there isn't even a DROP of reindeer poo on Walter's house!! **NOT A DROP!!**

This can only mean one thing . . .

I can barely bring myself to write it . . .

SANTA IS A SOFTY!!!

I just can't believe it . . . It's too, too horrible. Santa, a Softy?!?! I bet he even enjoys flower-arranging! I'll make sure to send him a copy of my Menacing Diary when I'm done. He clearly needs some serious help from me. He'll be playing tricks on his elves and leaving me the most presents in the world by the time I've finished with him.

Hmmm . . . Well, Santa was a whopping great no-hoper . . . At least I've got Gran . . . She always brings great presents.

Yep! Gran won't let me down. I'm off to watch cartoons until she arrives. That'll take my mind off the terrible news about Softy Santa . . .

2 p.m.: I can hear the sound of Gran's Charley Davidson motorbike . . . YEAH!!

SHE'S HERE AND SHE'S BROUGHT HER DOG GNIPPER AND HER PIG RASHER!!

YEEEEEAAAAAHHHHHH!!!!

2.10 p.m.: AMAZING! Gran got me a **MEGA-SQUIRT WATER BLASTER!!** This is going to be perfect for soaking Soggy-Softy-Pants-Walter next term. He's going to be even soggier than normal! I knew Gran wouldn't let me down . . .

3 p.m.: Sitting down to watch Christmas TV with Gran and Bea. Gnipper and Gnasher are having a great time digging holes through the snow in the back garden and Mum and Dad are getting on with the Christmas dinner . . . There's a really strange smell coming from the kitchen, though . . . kinda like burnt rubber . . . Hmmm . . . I dunno . . .

3.10 p.m.: Belching competition with Gran. We're seeing who can do the most Christmassy-smelling burp. Mine smelled like mince pies, but Gran definitely won . . . Her belch smelled like stuffing, roast potatoes AND Brussels sprouts all in one . . . It was **DISGUSTING!!** And she hasn't even eaten any of those things yet!! **She's so cool!!**

3.30 p.m.: MMMMMMMMM, CHRISTMAS DINNER TIME!! We just had to drag Rasher down from the top of the Christmas tree . . . HA! It was

HILARIOUS!

Mum didn't think and brought out a big roasted ham and Rasher went nuts! I wonder if he recognized it . . . Maybe it was his great-aunt Petunia or something?

Mum's furious. Rasher knocked all the ornaments off the tree and there are pine needles all over the carpet. He soon calmed down when Dad gave him a big bowl of potato peelings . . .

WHAT IS THAT SMELL???

3.37 p.m.: AAAAAGGGHH!!! That smell!! Mum just brought out the turkey and it stinks of rubber . . . **BEA'S DOLL!!** I COMPLETELY FORGOT TO GET IT BACK OUT . . . MUM ROASTED HER!!

3.42 p.m.: RUMBLED . . . Mum just found the remains of Little Baby Tinkle-Pants inside the turkey . . . She just went bananas and sent Bea to her room.

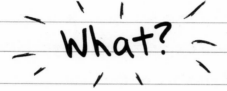

I'm not going to tell her it was me!!

Bea has a stash of biscuits and sweets under her bed anyway . . . She'll be fine.

For a scary moment, I thought Mum was going to still make us eat the **rubbery, stinking turkey** . . .

3.47 p.m.: YEAH!! DAD JUST CALLED BEANOTOWN BURGERS AND IT'S OPEN. BEANOTOWN BURGERS FOR CHRISTMAS DINNER!?!? YEAH, HE'S ORDERING TAKEAWAY. ONE SLOPPER–GNOSHER–GUT–BUSTIN' BURGER TO GO, PLEASE!

4.16 p.m.: I'm so happy . . . My burger is the best Christmas dinner I've ever had . . .

Gran ordered the Sizzlin'–Chilli–Tongue–Torture Burger . . . It's so spicy you can spit flames after eating it . . .

Ha! Gran singed Dad's eyebrows . . .

7.30 p.m.: What a brilliant day. I've got my Mega-Squirt Water Blaster and my belly is full of the best burger in Beanotown.

Mum and Dad stopped squabbling and actually seemed to enjoy their Super-Loop Chips, and Gnasher and Gnipper loved the rubbery turkey. They don't care if Little Baby Tinkle-Pants is melted all over it.

Gran is snoring in the armchair with her false teeth hanging halfway out of her mouth and everyone is happy . . .

This has turned out to be the
BEST
Christmas
ever!!

I can't believe the year is almost over . . . It's been a long old slog, eh?

I guess the only thing left to do is come up with a New Year's resolution for next term.

Hmmmm . . . .

- Try my hardest to be **good** . . .

- Eat my **vegetables** . . .

- Be nice to **Walter** . . .

- Make sure I do my **homework** on time . . .

UGH!

WHO AM I KIDDING?

NEVER
STOP
MENACING!!!

SEE YOU NEXT TERM,

MY MENACING MATES!

BAN THE
BUM-FACES!

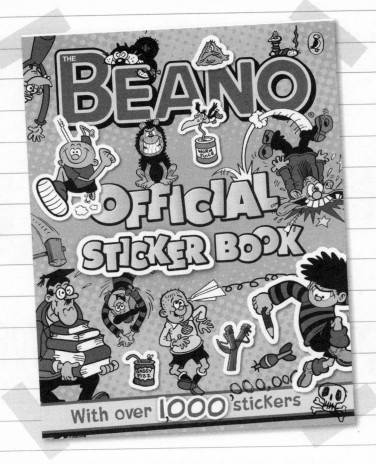

PS I'm going to buy this book too! Just
imagine where I could put all those stickers
of my menacing mates, Gnasher and me!
I think I'll start with decorating my diary . . .